I'M FUN, TOO!

Jonathan Fenske

Scholastic Inc.

To Pendy, Coco, and Lulu, the pieces that make the set complete!

ISBN 978-1-338-26097-7

10 9 8 7 6 5 4 3 2 1   18 19 20 21 22

Printed in China   62

First edition 2018

Look at the NEW guys . . .

. . . with their **FANCY HAIR,**

and **FANCY CLOTHES,**

and **FANCY FACES.**

Yep. Two dots and one line.
That's all I get.

happy

sad

mad

scared

Even when it REALLY HURTS.

Hmmmph. Not the FUN, NEW guys.

happy

sad

mad

scared

They LAUGH!

They SHOUT!

They SING!

I USED to have the best BIKE on the block.

Not anymore.

Let's face it. If we were ice cream . . .

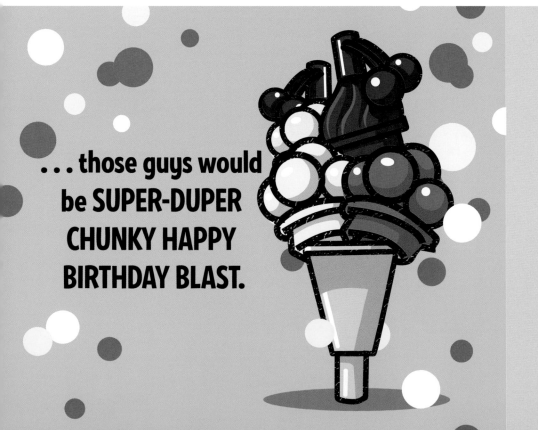

. . . those guys would be SUPER-DUPER CHUNKY HAPPY BIRTHDAY BLAST.

And I would be VANILLA.

But I'm like a blank sheet of paper!

I'm like an empty canvas!

I can be whomever I WANT to be!

Give me a SWORD and I'll save the day!

Give me a ROCKET
and I'll reach the stars!